GARFIELD
The Big Star

Created by Jim Davis
Story by Norma Simone

Originally published as *GARFIELD The Fussy Cat*

A GOLDEN BOOK • NEW YORK

Western Publishing Company, Inc., Racine, Wisconsin 53404

One sunny day Garfield sat in the window, looking at the world outside. He saw bees gathering nectar from the flowers. He saw birds building a nest. He saw squirrels chasing each other through the trees.

"It's a pretty day," Garfield thought. He yawned. "Pretty boring, that is."

"How can I beat this boredom?" Garfield asked himself. "I know! I'll tie Odie's ears in a knot!"

So Garfield tied Odie's ears in a knot. But it wasn't much fun, because Odie was too dumb even to notice.

"Dumb dog, dumb day," said Garfield.

"Jon, I need some excitement in my life," said Garfield.

Jon Arbuckle looked up from his newspaper. "Listen to this, Garfield," he said. "Fussy Cat Brand Cat Food is looking for a cat to star in a TV commercial. They're holding auditions today."

"How terribly uninteresting," said Garfield.

"The cat they choose gets a year's supply of Fussy Cat Brand Cat Food," said Jon.

"I'd rather have lasagna," said Garfield.

"Plus a year-long, all-expense-paid trip around the world," said Jon.

"A trip around the world! That's the kind of excitement I need! Let's go!" Garfield said, dragging Jon toward the door.

Garfield and Jon went to the TV studio.

"We're here to audition for the Fussy Cat commercial," Jon told the secretary.

"Tell the Fussy Cat people that their new star has arrived," said Garfield.

"Get in line," said the secretary.

There must have been a hundred owners and their cats waiting to audition for the commercial. Garfield and Jon were at the end of the line.

"A star like me should not have to wait," said Garfield.

So Garfield thought of a great trick.

He leaned over to the cat next to him.

"Say, did you hear about that accident over on Main Street?" said Garfield loudly. "A truck full of fresh fish and a truck full of cream both flipped over. Main Street is one gigantic lunch!"

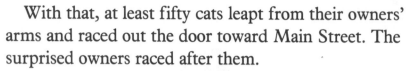
With that, at least fifty cats leapt from their owners'
arms and raced out the door toward Main Street. The
surprised owners raced after them.

"What's going on?" said Jon.

"Guess they were afraid to face the camera," said
Garfield with a smile.

An assistant director asked Jon some questions. "Does your cat have any special talents?" he asked.

"Just eating and sleeping," said Jon. "Oh, and he does a great imitation of an orange beach ball," he added, laughing.

"Remind me to shred your favorite chair when we get home," Garfield said to Jon.

Finally there was just one more cat ahead of Garfield. Garfield watched him audition. In front of the camera was a bowl of Fussy Cat Brand Cat Food. Beside the bowl was a big bag filled with more Fussy Cat Brand Cat Food. The cat walked up to the bowl, smiled at the camera, and began to eat neat little mouthfuls.

Garfield jumped from Jon's arms and raced onto the stage. "This commercial isn't big enough for both of us," said Garfield, bumping the other cat aside.

Garfield flashed the director a big smile. "You want a cat who can eat?" Garfield asked. "I'll show you a cat who can eat!"

Garfield picked up the bowl of Fussy Cat Brand Cat Food, flipped the food into his mouth, and swallowed it in one gulp!

"Amazing!" said the director.

But Garfield didn't stop there. He ripped open the big bag of Fussy Cat Brand Cat Food and began pouring the food into his mouth. In an instant he had finished the entire bag.

"Incredible!" shouted the director. "We've found our Fussy Cat!"

"Burp," said Garfield.

The director planned to shoot the commercial that
very afternoon. There was a lot of preparation to do.
First he brought in a hairdresser for Garfield.

"Just trim a little off the tummy," said Garfield.

At the same time a manicurist filed and polished
Garfield's claws.

Then the wardrobe people brushed Garfield's fur until it was smooth and shiny. Garfield purred happily.

"This is the life," thought Garfield. "The bright lights, the cameras, the excitement—I was born to be a star!"

"This is great, Garfield," said Jon. "Thanks to you, we'll soon be off on a year-long trip around the world!"

"Oh, I'm sorry, Mr. Arbuckle," said the director. "Only Garfield will be going on our world tour. But we do have a nice Fussy Cat Brand Cat Food calendar for you."

"Gee, thanks," said Jon sadly.

"I'll send you a postcard," said Garfield.

Now Garfield was having second thoughts about his new, exciting life. He hadn't counted on being apart from Jon and Odie for a whole year. He thought of all the dumb things Odie would do in a year, and all the dumb things Jon would say. Garfield would miss all that.

"It's tough being a star," said Garfield. "Fortunately, I'm big enough to handle it."

It was time to start filming.

"Here's all your cat has to do," the director said to Jon. "He goes to the bowl marked 'Brand X,' sniffs it, and walks away. He does the same thing with the bowl marked 'Brand Y.' But when he comes to the bowl marked 'Fussy Cat,' he gobbles it down. Any questions?"

"When do I get my nap break?" said Garfield with a yawn.

"Places, everybody," said the director.
"And...ACTION!"

Garfield walked up to the "Brand X" cat food. He
sniffed it and walked away.

"Good, good," said the director.

Then Garfield sniffed the "Brand Y" cat food and
walked away.

"Excellent, excellent," said the director.

Finally Garfield came to the Fussy Cat Brand Cat Food. He sniffed it carefully. He leaned closer to the bowl. He opened his mouth.

"That's it. That's it," said the director.

Suddenly Garfield felt *very* full and *very* sleepy. "I think I overdid my audition," he said. And with that he fell fast asleep—facedown—in the food!

"CUT! CUT!" yelled the director.

That night Jon fixed Garfield a special lasagna dinner. "You know, Garfield," said Jon, "I'm glad you didn't make that commercial. Odie and I would have missed you."

"BARK!" said Odie in agreement.

"I guess the part wasn't right for me," said Garfield. But he didn't really mind not being the star of a commercial. "After all," he said, "I'll always be the biggest star in this house!"